MW01173260

WITH PARKINSON'S

The First Two Years

Edward Boss Wood

Bernard, Maine

ISBN

DEDICATION

To Stephen L. Guinn – a modern Druid.

His wisdom and calm were an inspiration.

TABLE OF CONTENTS

PART III: LOOKING FORWARD

PREFACE

This short book contains my reminiscences from the first two years after I received a diagnosis of Parkinson's disease. I kept a diary at the time, and, at the suggestion of friends, have turned my thoughts from that time into this book. My hope is that it will be a help to others facing the same challenges. Fourteen years have passed, and I am still going strong, albeit more slowly, with greater dependence on the people around me. I hope to write about my more recent experiences with this disease, but in this short volume, I have concentrated on the beginning.

In the fourteen interim years, I have made a number of intimate friends who share this diagnosis. We have many things in common- but no single common path. However, we share the experience that the initial adaptation is a very tough phase, where fears and dreads can dominate. And part of that is coming face to face with mortality.

My first experience with the disease was a lonely one. The impulse to withdraw from social interaction is strong. Overcoming that impulse is an important aspect of moving forward. I learned much from this tough phase, and find I share with friends with this disease many common experiences. We have the challenge of coming to terms with the illness, returning to enjoyment of life, and the love of family and friends. My hope is that my experiences will be a help to others living through these challenges. You need to say goodbye to the healthy person who you were - and prepare to come to terms with the new direction life is taking, the new person you are becoming.

Edward Boss Wood

PART I: THE BEGINNING

August 2011. The August sun in Maine was warm. On particularly pleasant days, I would take a break after lunch to sit in the sun at the corner of our porch. During just such a break, I noticed a tremor in my right hand. There was no pain, and the tremor was slight. I had noticed it a few times before. I counted it as yet another reminder of my approaching sixtieth birthday and gave it little further thought. A few weeks later we closed the house, stowed the porch furniture and returned to our home in Pittsburgh, where I had worked for thirty-five years as a lawyer, and where we raised our three children.

September 2011. I had my annual physical in mid-September. At the end of the exam, I mentioned the tremor as I dressed to leave. My doctor responded by asking me to do some simple hand and finger movements and to walk down the hall. He did not share any concerns but referred me to a neurologist. His reaction carried no sense of urgency. I could have pushed for more information, but on some level, I was not anxious to learn more. I called the neurologist's office when I returned home. The first appointment by the University of Pittsburgh Medical Center (UPMC) Neurology Department was over four months away. Whatever I had, it apparently did not require prompt attention. I made my appointment and did my best to ignore the tremor.

February 2012 On the day of the appointment, I found my neurologist's office in the patchwork of medical office buildings that make up UPMC's Oakland campus. The neurology department was in the midst of office renovations and could only be reached by way of a bewildering series of elevators and corridors. The waiting room was not yet finished, so patients waited in chairs that lined the hall. In due course, the neurologist came into the hall, introduced himself and led me to an exam room where we were joined by his physician's assistant. The exam that followed was brief and anachronistically simple. I rotated my feet and hands, tapped my fingers, and walked down the hall and back, much as I had done at my annual physical in September.

When I returned to the exam room from my excursion down the hallway, I expected to be told that we would begin the series of sophisticated and expensive tests that seem to have become in recent years the hallmark of encounters with the medical world. I was wrong. Employing warm professional tones and simple phrases particularly appropriate for the neurologically impaired, my neurologist told me that there was an 85% chance that I had Parkinson's disease. He said there is no cure, and the cause was likewise uncertain. Drugs currently in use simply masked symptoms, which he did not describe. There were no new drugs of any significance in the pipeline. The disease would progress very slowly and might not require drug therapy for as much as five years. He then described at length expensive tests that would increase the accuracy of the diagnosis, but the results of these tests would not be of much use because their outcome would not change the course of my treatment.

I remember no strong emotions on hearing the diagnosis. I understood the words and accepted the diagnosis as if the words were not, on some level, entirely a surprise. I declined the offered second opinion and I declined the expensive tests, seeing no real point. As we wrapped up, the neurologist cautioned me not to research the disease on the Internet.

By the time I left the office, my thoughts were confused and edged with fear. Ten minutes earlier, I had expected to commence a series of tests, perhaps focused on a mild concussion I had had a year or so before, culminating in some extended and possibly effective therapy. I never imagined that my first visit would end with diagnosis of an incurable neurodegenerative disease. While I understood the actual words, I had no real comprehension of my new reality. I had planned to go to my downtown office after the appointment, but by the time I found my way to the street, it seemed pointless to go back to work. The winter air was cold, but the sun was bright. Walking has always calmed me. I decided to walk the three miles back to our townhouse and try to enjoy the remains of the day.

As I walked toward home my mind kept returning to my new five-year window. Nearly sixty and in good health, I had thought before the exam that I might reasonably have a twenty-year window of active health. Now an assumption that had informed my life had evaporated in a moment. I convinced myself, after walking a mile or so, that five years was far enough in the future to justify postponing, at least for the time being, further thoughts of my mortality, and I began to think about Parkinson's itself. I have known about the disease for years, but I knew none of its symptoms beyond the tremor universally associated with the disease. Despite my doctor's advice, I decided to take a quick look at the Internet, and I pulled out my phone.

I quickly learned why Internet research was a bad idea. Wikipedia informed the inquiring reader that Parkinson's is a progressive and incurable degenerative neurological disease. My tremor would increase, and my mobility and muscle control would decline. I would likely suffer progressive cognitive impairment, and eventual dementia. My swallowing would be disrupted, increasing the risk of aspirating food and developing pneumonia. I would lose control of my facial muscles, which might be good for poker (I don't play), but was decidedly not good for animated conversation, which I relish. Digestion could be incomplete and painful. Incontinence and impotence lurked in the shadows, and I was warned ominously to guard against constipation. In short, many of the medical conditions that I had considered mildly or seriously alarming were on my horizon, and my horizon was now only five years out.

For the remainder of my walk home, I tried with mixed success not to dwell on the future. When I arrived home, my wife Janet was out. I walked Nell, our dog, sat down in our family room and resolved to share the diagnosis with Janet calmly and dispassionately. When she did return, I tried to be stoic, but I cried before I finished my first sentence. Then we cried together.

The Rest of my Life began the next morning. I awoke the next morning much as I had awakened every other day in the recent past. Nothing had changed in the 18 hours since the diagnosis. I had no new symptoms. My tremor was intermittent. Still, everything had changed. I would never again wake to a day without Parkinson's. My symptoms might not worsen quickly, but the disease was not going away. My condition would continue to deteriorate, however slowly.

I faced no questions about the course of my immediate treatment. There was no immediate treatment and no cure. Even though everything had changed, there was nothing that had to be done for what might be months or even years. I had no immediate financial pressure. My insurance and savings would replace my work income for the next five years and provide for a comfortable retirement even after the added expense of coping with the disease. Aside from my work, I was left with only one immediate decision. Who to tell and how?

I suspect that some husbands and wives do not discuss their Parkinson's diagnosis with their families until their symptoms can no longer be concealed. They keep their secret and ignore or suppress their fear as best they can, and for some with symptoms, silence may hold the promise of quelling or at least postponing the terrors that lurk in an unknowable future. I never considered keeping the diagnosis from my wife Janet, even for a few days. My health has a very real impact on Janet's life. For this reason alone, she needed to know, and she had a right to know. And even if I had wanted to conceal my diagnosis for a few weeks or months, not telling her was hardly an option. I had long lost the ability to keep anything important from her, if I ever had it. Not telling her would have made it far more difficult for both of us to face my new situation. Janet needed time to absorb and process this new reality as much as I did, and we needed to process it together. By working together, each of us could serve as an emotional support and reality check to the other.

Telling our three children was a different matter. My failing health might in time provoke a crisis in their lives, but my health would not impact them the way it would impact Janet. There were no compelling reasons to tell them everything immediately. I knew that parents often conceal serious medical conditions from their children. Motives vary. Some may not wish to discuss with their children a disease that makes them afraid lest their children observe their fear and judge them for it.

Others may find potential disability a source of embarrassment. No one relishes the change in family relationships brought about by a disease that looks so much like weakness. As a father, I never want to appear weak or feeble in the eyes of my children. Thinking back to my youth in the late sixties, I realized that my own parents would have kept a diagnosis of Parkinson's from me and my brother for as long as they could. That's how many parents of their generation handled disturbing news. Perhaps their memories of the depression and my father's combat service were so difficult that they were determined to make their home a haven for their children. Perhaps they could not face their own fear. Whatever their reasons, they carefully avoided all disturbing topics. Having lived with my parent's protective secrecy as a child and young adult, I was convinced that secrecy was a bad idea. My children might not sense the subject of my concealment, but they would quickly grasp the fact that something had been concealed. On some level they would sense that something had changed and that our communications were in some way circumscribed, just as I had sensed concealment by my own parents. The disease would be an aspect of myself that I was not sharing, and the limitation on my sharing would be evident, even if the substance of the concealment were not. I might be able to conceal the diagnosis from them for a few years, but I could not completely conceal its shadow. The shadow would darken our relationships, and when the truth was ultimately known, they would have had every reason to feel the same pain that I might have hoped to postpone, combined now with a sense of betrayal and lost years of intimacy that could have been used to face the reality of the disease.

Releasing the cat from the bag slowly. It never made sense to Janet or me to keep the diagnosis from our children. We likewise agreed that the news was too important to share by telephone. A telephone call is an easy way to share bad news with adult children. It would avoid the pain of seeing the full impact of the news again in their faces, but it would limit the comfort we could give in person. It is hard to hear bad news, but it is easier to hear it face to face. Hugs simply don't work on a telephone. In years past, we have often taken a family trip in late winter in search of warm weather and uninterrupted, happy time together. In 2012, the year of my diagnosis, we had a stay in a rental house in the Bahamas planned for a week at the end of February. Our trip would begin only a few weeks after the diagnosis. It would provide an excellent opportunity to speak to each face to face.

I had not worried too much about the prospect of discussing my Parkinson's with my children, but when our vacation week finally arrived and we were in the Bahamas, I found myself procrastinating. I did not relish the conversation. Half the week passed before Janet's strong urging and the certainty that no better opportunity would likely arise made further avoidance impossible. I selected an evening when we expected dinner out. I planned to approach each of them as soon as they had finished dressing. If everything went as planned, each would have a moment alone with me while they were still absorbing the news. These short conversations would be followed by time together as a family, where, hopefully, no one would feel under pressure to talk or not.

Thankfully, the plan unfolded without untoward surprises. I succeeded in finding private opportunities to speak with each of the children in the hour leading up to dinner. The conversations were short; I told them about my five-year window and my regret that it was not longer. I told them that I loved them, and we hugged. I did not see pain in their eyes, as I had feared. Instead, each of them expressed their love and sympathy in their own characteristic way and each made it clear that they wanted to be a support for me. My expectations of their pain turned out to be projections of my own feelings that had little to do with their emotional state. There were tears, but they were good tears, and mostly mine. When we rejoined our family group for dinner, Parkinson's was not a topic of conversation.

The remaining few days of our vacation were, for me at least, flavored with relief. My delay in speaking with my children had caused me more anxiety than I had realized, and that anxiety had dissipated with our conversations. We did not talk about Parkinson's very much after that Thursday. We did talk about spending more time together and simply enjoyed being with each other. If anything, sharing my Parkinson's made our remaining time together more precious. We returned to our respective homes with plans for shared travel and family visits, all of which were in some way possible because of our Thursday conversations. Telling had been good.

Beyond the family? By the time Janet and I returned home to Pittsburgh, we had told all of our immediate families and our closest friends. We had not told a broader audience. While telling family and close friends seemed entirely right, the wisdom of telling others was not as clear. There were real reasons to keep my condition confidential. A close friend and colleague of mine survived cancer for nearly 25 years. He never told me about his disease, and I doubt that he told any but his closest colleagues and family members. We never discussed his reasons, even when he was obviously dying, but his decision was not hard to understand. Beyond his strong personal preference for privacy, it is difficult to work as a lawyer with a known serious disease. Even if the disease is not yet evident, health can deteriorate quickly, and clients do not want a lawyer who might not complete their projects or whose powers might be waning even if their fears are objectively unfounded. Talking about my Parkinson's freely and openly would certainly make it difficult to continue to work even part time.

Motivated by concerns about the possible backlash of disclosure, I initially chose to treat my condition as a private matter. In the months following our family vacation I rarely spoke to anyone outside the family about my Parkinson's. When I did mention the disease, the resulting conversation was often unsettling. Those in the business of being empathetic (such as clerics and health care workers) typically lowered their voices to express their profound concern. These conversations could be disturbing, because I did not feel that my observable symptoms warranted such a serious reaction. I worried that they might be anticipating problems of which I was blissfully unaware, or worse, that my symptoms were more obvious than I thought and warranted pity. Other listeners were indifferent, probably because they did not understand the disease. Some betrayed their own fear as they deflected my comment with cheerful but empty encouragement. Very few people knew me well enough or were compassionate enough to give me any real comfort.

These experiences seemed to confirm my decision not to talk about my disease to any but family and a few trusted friends. In time, however, I would grow to question the wisdom of this decision.

My voice. For nearly a year before my diagnosis, I was often hoarse and could not speak as clearly or as loudly as I wished. It was hard to make myself heard on the phone or in groups. This was a problem in court, where microphones are not commonly on and where volume can sometimes be used by an opponent as a substitute for logic. If I could not make myself heard, I could not be an effective advocate for my clients. As my voice grew increasingly feeble, it also began to impact my social life. I was often overlooked in conversations that involved multiple speakers. My timing was off. I found myself trying to be heard a few moments after the conversation had moved beyond the point I wished to interject. When I tried harder, I spoke too loudly or interrupted the flow of conversation. When I gave up, the conversation passed me by. In time, my hoarseness progressed to the point that I could not make a voicemail recording on my phone that did not telegraph that something was wrong. A client suggested that I change my message because he thought it sounded like I was dying.

Breathing. Another problem that had emerged at this time was a return of asthma. As a child, I had several isolated asthma attacks that frightened me at the time but had largely disappeared by the time I went to college. Asthma returned in my late twenties, but it was easily controlled by medication and the avoidance of allergens. However, about a year before my Parkinson's diagnosis, my asthma returned with a new intensity, and this time, it was paired at times with a palpable, instinctual fear, not unlike my first experience with asthma as a child. Medication did not seem to help. An extended, uncontrollable spell of restricted breathing ultimately brought me to the emergency room. Subsequent tests showed that my lung capacity was significantly diminished. New drugs, including smaller particle steroids, would gradually help, but the visceral fear remained.

Vision. Around the time I was dealing with my asthma, I also found that I could not work at a computer for more than an hour without blurred vision. A visit to my ophthalmologist disclosed that I had cataracts in both eyes. Two surgeries removed the cataracts, but my vision was slow to return and vision in my left eye stayed blurred. I could not work full days after my operation. I concluded (incorrectly) that my vision problems were yet another chapter of aging. I did not connect my vision problems with Parkinson's until months later.

Stress tolerance A few weeks before my Parkinson's diagnosis, a client called while I was away in Hawaii to ask me to return to testify at an emergency hearing a few hours north of Pittsburgh. I responded promptly. I boarded a red-eye flight back home and drove north into a winter storm. I arrived at the courthouse well before the hearing, but I began to shake and shiver violently as the time for my testimony approached. The shaking left me flustered and unsure of myself. I was more than relieved when my testimony turned out to be unnecessary. By that evening, I had calmed and largely regained my composure. I attributed my shaking to the abrupt cold and the rigors of stressful travel. Had I been more attentive, I might have recognized that this was only another instance of my growing inability to cope with stress.

The next months. During the months after the diagnosis, symptoms kept coming. My tremor worsened quickly, spreading to my right leg. The shaking now interrupted my concentration. Sometimes, I had an internal tremor. I felt like I was shaking violently but was in fact quite still. I often braced my legs against a chair or a wall to control them when I was sitting. My leg tremor undercut my physical confidence. I grew tentative and uncertain of my footing. I no longer swung my arms when I walked, and my balance suffered as a result. My energy levels dropped perceptibly, even though I had continued to exercise and follow my diet. Tasks that would have taken hours now took days. As spring approached, I often only had enough energy to exercise, open my mail, pay my bills and go home for a late afternoon nap. I rarely awoke from the nap refreshed. My thought was often slow and muddled. I knew that I was not always thinking clearly, but I could not always differentiate between clarity and confusion.

I became increasingly sensitive to loud noises. Dinner at noisy restaurants became a trial because I could not hear or be heard. Kitchen noises were grating and stressful. Dining out was less and less enjoyable, while the volume at movie theaters was physically painful. I had a recurrent ringing in my ears and my hearing was less acute. I found myself increasingly unwilling to take risks or pursue new experiences. I began to find it increasingly difficult to get up from bed. I was sometimes trapped by bedclothes that had entangled me during the night. I had an urgent need to urinate that woke me several times each night. Nocturnal visits to the bathroom grew perilous. If I could escape my blankets and sheets, I was still tentative as I walked unsteadily toward the toilet.

My urgent need to urinate continued to arise unpredictably during the day. When I rushed (or, more accurately, lurched) toward the men's room, shirttails and the contents of my pocket added their own fiendish impediments to the accomplishment of the pressing task before me. If I thought about urinating as I walked home from the bus, I often had a real challenge getting home to the bathroom in time. Several times I didn't quite make it, and I began to favor dark pants just in case. I dreaded the day when I wouldn't make it at all.

Chapter 4: The Fight with Shame and Fear: Old Coping Strategies Don't Work

Shame takes root. Soon after the diagnosis, I realized that I had become ashamed of my Parkinson's. I knew that shame was irrational. There is nothing about Parkinson's that justifies shame, (even the growing risk of incontinence!). Still, I felt ashamed. Parkinson's offended my pride and contradicted my long-held self-image. It seemed to be transforming me from a vital, energetic, self-assured lawyer, husband and father into an increasingly vulnerable, tentative and diminished sixty-year old. I had only grudgingly accepted middle age, and now I had many of the characteristics of an old man. I was abashed by what I was becoming. I began to withdraw into myself. I started to question whether I could make a meaningful contribution to any conversation. I felt no longer interesting or attractive. My universe seemed to shrink. A gulf was opening separating me from the wider world.

Fear visits for a long stay. My blurred vision also triggered fear, but of a different sort. I could tolerate blurred vision for a time, but the prospect of permanent vision loss was a source of gnawing worry. My continued work as a trial lawyer, my appreciation of art and literature, my avocations of photography and travel would all be more difficult if not impossible if my vision deteriorated further. From the moment of my Parkinson's diagnosis, fear was never far from the surface. Parkinson's was a blank sheet of paper that could be filled with any fear my mind could conjure. The fear of

Parkinson's was neither the visceral fear of an asthma attack nor the gnawing anxiety aroused by my worsening vision. It was an unpredictable fear that arose in the night as the concerns of the day subsided. It was a fear that came into my mind uncontrollably and unpredictably at times of its own choosing. Within a week after my diagnosis, I found myself awake in a cold sweat at two in the morning gripped by an intense fear that would remain with me for hours. These late-night visitations continued.

Behind and below the physical symptoms and the tough hope for a defense against this disease lay the deeper fears of mortality. My father died suddenly from an aneurism soon after his sixty-seventh birthday. I would soon be sixty. Might my life be shorter than I had come to assume? My mother lived much longer than my father, but the last decade of her life saw her slipping inexorably into dementia. Was this to be my fate? Would my five-year window be plagued by new health issues and be followed by a steady decline into dementia? In the weeks following my diagnosis, Janet read to me from the Psalms at the end of each day in hopes of calming my anxiety. It was pleasant to listen to and it helped: her voice and presence always calmed me, but this time, it did not resolve my fear. I prayed, but prayers did not bring the respite that I so desperately sought. I recalled a verse from the Gospel of John. "Perfect love casts out fear." The verse was more perplexing than helpful. What was perfect love? My love for Janet and my children was apparently insufficient to cast out my fear, and my love for God was likewise inadequate. God's love for me and my family was by definition perfect, but it did not cast out my fear. As I thought more about it, the verse was not a comfort, but rather seemed to taunt me as I tried unsuccessfully to cope with my fear.

Time and greater focus on my family and others around me partly dulled my anxiety, but it did not go away. Fear would continue to haunt me, and still can surprise me in the early morning hours. My fear continued just beneath the surface. But in these first months, I really could not yet face the reality of my disease or what felt like my impending death. I felt that I was not ready; that I needed more time with my new reality before I could face my fear.

Old Coping Strategies Stopped Working. I briefly considered the possibility of treating my Parkinson's as an opponent. Many cancer patients find hope and motivation by treating their disease as a personal battle. Lance Armstrong and his "live strong" campaign come to mind. Armstrong and others tell us that we can beat our illnesses if only we are resolute enough, strong enough, and committed enough to fight. This attitude may help many some people facing challenging illnesses, particularly if there is a chance of recovery. The strategy was not helpful for me, however, because it could only be based on assumptions I knew to be false. Ultimately, I cannot "win." There is no way for me to "beat" my Parkinson's. Absent a true medical miracle, I will still have Parkinson's on the day I die. If I consider my Parkinson's as my opponent, I must also accept the fact that my opponent will ultimately prevail. How can I mobilize for a war that I know I will lose?

Since I could not ignore the disease, for a while I tried another strategy, that I called "*stoic acceptance*". Stoic acceptance seemed at first a reasonable attitude to take in the face of an incurable disease. My fate was set; there was no point in resisting the irresistible. Moreover, I admire displays of quiet strength in the face of conflicts, setbacks, and tragedies, so stoic acceptance appealed to my vanity. Stoic acceptance may indeed be inspiring when we encounter it in movies and literature, but with further thought I came to realize that it was a dangerous way for me to face a degenerative illness. My father ignored his own symptoms of serious vascular disease until he was forced to the hospital with intractable pain. He never returned home. He was sixty-seven. There are many similar stories. Whether as a result of fear, a misplaced concept of personal strength or an irrational commitment to their work, many men and women ignore symptoms of serious illnesses and die prematurely of treatable diseases. Stoic acceptance born of denial masquerades as strength, but it is often motivated by fear, and it all too often leads to a passivity that deprives us of the help we need.

Uncomplaining acceptance did not work for me because acceptance meant embracing the inevitability of my deterioration. Since we are told that our deterioration is linear, irreversible and progressive, quiet acceptance of my disease meant acceptance of the fact that each year, each month, each week, will be worse than the one before.

If this is true, where can I find hope? If there is no hope, how can I keep my fear at bay? What is the point of resisting if I am only postponing the inevitable? If I accepted my Parkinson's and all its implications, how could I keep my fear of what it will bring tomorrow from engulfing me today?

The limits of stoic acceptance. Although stoicism did nothing to reduce my fear, it did feed my depression, and my depression made it difficult to muster the will to contain my fear. Acceptance of my fate seemed unlikely to free me to enjoy my remaining days. At best, it seemed like it would only prepare me for my inevitable death. Coping strategies are useful if they give us the hope and courage we need to challenge each other or help contain our fear. To confront fear, hope must be grounded in reality. Acceptance of my disease gave me nothing to hope for, while treating my disease as a mortal enemy would ignore the facts of my predicament. Each of these strategies was based on a fallacy, and thus are not likely to give me any real and lasting hope. By default, I decided to avoid thinking about the disease for the immediate future. Hardly a strategy, but I suspect that most people kick the question of mortality down the road for most of their lives.

Thinking about my work as a lawyer was in the background this whole time. Lawyers do many things, but all of them involve stress and confrontations. The work of a trial lawyer can be particularly stressful. Deadlines are a constant worry. Clients resist advice and challenge invoices. Adversaries resist demands with the assistance of aggressive lawyers. Judges resist everyone. All of my professional communications involved the potential for stress, and even the most innocuous of conversation could devolve unexpectedly into a heated disagreement. Stress was particularly toxic to me as my Parkinson's continued to evolve. When my stress levels rose, my ability to think and express myself plummeted. I had limited my practice due to my vision problems long before my diagnosis. I was working part time, but even so I was often undone by the confusion and shaking that accompanied even mild stress. By May, I could no longer ignore the fact that my Parkinson's not only made me easily exhausted and sometimes miserable, it also slowed and muddled my thinking. I had begun to realize that my days as a lawyer might be over. I began to come to recognize that I was, for lack of a better word, disabled.

After my childhood dreams of becoming an archeologist faded, I wanted to be a lawyer. At first, it was my father's idea. He may have wanted me to pursue his own thwarted dreams of becoming a lawyer, or he may have seen potential in me at an early age. Whatever his reason, I didn't have a better idea. I liked intellectual challenges. Arguments and strategy always engaged me.

I enjoyed the challenge of solving complex problems and I liked writing. I never regretted my choice of profession. I thoroughly enjoyed being a lawyer, even while complaining about the merciless demands of hourly billing and the vicissitudes of client relationships. While I worked almost exclusively for businesses, I had enough financial freedom as the owner of a successful commercial firm to help people when opportunities arose and to select engagements that interested me.

Over the course of thirty-four years, I had handled litigation throughout the United States and Europe, worked with some very talented people, participated in some important cases and had a lot of fun along the way. My practice had given me financial independence and the ability to choose cases and clients. I saw myself as a lawyer and expected to continue be a lawyer for the rest of my life. Now, that expectation was fading but I was completely unprepared for retirement psychologically. I had no plan, no sport, no consuming hobby, no bucket list, and no thoughts of a second career. I had no idea how I would spend my time or find a way to live a meaningful life. My professional life had involved stress levels that I would never be able to tolerate again, but it also gave my life a familiar rhythm and simplifying focus. I had enjoyed the people I met and took great pleasure in engaging and challenging work. I knew that on most normal workdays when not traveling I would be at my desk by eight, exercise at lunch and be home by seven. I had no need to ask whether my work was worthwhile because it was important to my clients and it paid my bills.

That spring, my new normal workday was very different from my normal workdays of the past. My days were no longer tightly scheduled. Having curtailed my work to cope with my vision problems and early Parkinson's symptoms, clients were no longer clambering for attention. With limited billable work, most of my time in the office was dedicated to returning, securing or shredding hundreds of closed files that I had accumulated over years. While this work was not demanding, I still only had enough energy and periods of mental clarity to work a handful of hours each week. Progress was exceedingly slow, but the file work allowed me to postpone the troubling question of what I would do next.

By May, I increasingly felt that I was no longer a full member of the healthy workday world, although not yet ready to close up shop. I was still a lawyer, but healthy colleagues did not understand my new physical and intellectual limitations, and I no longer cared nearly as much about the day-to-day world that I had shared with them only a short time before. I was uncomfortable with other lawyers because my practice gave me nothing new or interesting to talk about. I knew that when I could no longer practice law, I would need to find a new calling, but for the time being I postponed this problem.

As the winter of 2012 gave way to spring, I came to realize that there was no simple strategy that would allow me to deal with the reality of my disease and my fears. I continued to be an inadvertent Stoic, turning to dark humor for a release. I told friends that I had rats in my brain that were randomly eating the insulation off my wires. While disturbing to some, my dark humor was also my first step toward my subjective understanding of the disease. I continued to pray and attend church. I read as widely as I always had, although less frequently, for shorter periods, and at a much slower pace. I exercised regularly, practiced yoga, and ate balanced, regular meals. I avoided stress as best I could, limiting work to no more than an hour or two each day. I knew that I had Janet's constant love and the support and the encouragement of my family and friends. Still my depression lingered, seemingly unabated, magnifying the impact of my symptoms and narrowing the scope of my world.

A second neurologist opinion When I was first diagnosed in late February, my neurologist offered to arrange a second opinion. At the time, I saw this as unnecessary, but Janet and several close friends frequently urged me to reconsider. By early April, I finally overcame my reluctance to ask questions that frightened me. With help from a good friend, I arranged a meeting with Tim Greenamyre, the chief of UPMC's neurodegenerative disorders division and a leading

Parkinson's researcher. Tim examined me and we spent the best part of an hour discussing the disease and my potential future. Tim reiterated that the disease progressed slowly. He indicated that I might have an active life for 20 years, albeit one supported by medication. He approved of exercise, a balanced diet, rest and stress avoidance. He did not disapprove of coenzyme Q10, a dietary supplement which some think may slow Parkinson's. After all, even though CoQ10's neurological benefits are largely unproven, its cardiac benefits are not.

When I mentioned my vision problems, Tim told me that my occasional difficulty in focusing my left eye was probably caused by my Parkinson's. If that is the case, the problem will not go away as I had hoped. Oddly, I was relieved. Now I was free to make the best of what was likely permanent. My meeting with Tim helped me move one more step toward acceptance of the fact that my fear of imminent deterioration was not baked-in reality. I was still afraid, but I also knew that I still had a life to live. I still had obligations to my friends and family. Tim is by all accounts a superb scientist and a great hope for Parkinson's treatment. Thankfully, he was willing to speak factually and eschewed any attempt to project professional empathy. Still, the facts we discussed were comforting in ways that empathy would not have been. I needed to hear about my disease calmly, dispassionately, and accurately.

My introduction to neuropsychology. By early May, following the wise advice from Janet, I finally admitted to myself that I needed help with my depression and met with my primary care physician to discuss the problem. Wisely, he did not immediately prescribe an antidepressant. Instead, he recommended that I meet with a neuropsychologist, Douglass Reiss, Ph.D., to discuss the physical and emotional aspects of my disease before starting medication. I made the appointment right away, although only vaguely aware of neuropsychology as a research discipline, and with no firm idea about what sort of therapy a neuropsychologist might provide.

I met Dr. Reiss at his office. After shaking hands, he directed me to sit on a sofa opposite his chair. I sank into deep, well-used cushions with the fleeting concern that I might not be able to escape at the end of the session. Dr. Reiss began by assuring me that, despite the couch-like sofa, we would not be exploring my psyche or my childhood. Rather, he would become my mentor and coach as I worked to face the realities of my disease and its symptoms. He began by discussing the symptoms I could expect as the disease progressed. Describing frightening things in a matter of fact way helps to drain fear. I would have trouble walking and would lose mobility, but I could adapt, at least at first, as millions of people have done in the past. My periods of confusion would return, but it would not be permanent for a long time, if at all. I would have problems with my voice and hearing, but I could compensate by avoiding crowds and noise. I would continue to have a sense of losing myself from time to time, but I would still be me.

Doug's conversations with me were not rushed. We would often discuss a single issue over several sessions. Doug would probe areas where I was not forthcoming and could identify concerns I had about the disease and my future that I avoided, whether from fear or simple confusion. My neurologists, impeded by time constraints imposed by insurance reimbursement and the tremendous demand for their services, did not have the time necessary to identify, let alone explore, fears and concerns that I concealed even from myself. Doug's help, while not covered by insurance, was invaluable. Far from frightening me, my discussions with Doug about the facts helped me to begin the process of making a new life adapted to my developing disease. My old life was over, but perhaps a new life could be built. My daughter Emily, a child life specialist who frequently works with terminally ill children, calls it "a new normal."

Doug somewhat cryptically told me in one of our early sessions that everything had changed for me, but nothing had changed. At first this observation seemed to be either a bit obvious or a bit cliché. However, as I repeatedly turned my mind to this simple phrase, I began to understand some of its intended meaning. Perhaps in time I would cope with my new, challenging symptoms as they presented themselves, face my fears as they arose, and live my life each day as best I am able, just as I had done in the past.

I mused about Doug's statement that everything had changed for me, but nothing had changed. One morning, I awoke with the image in my mind of a close friend, thirty years my senior. We had known each other for many years, and the years had fostered a quiet, supportive mutual affection. His image did not give me any special insight into perfect love, and I doubt that he would consider himself to be an example, but the mere thought of him seemed to calm me. His steady support, along with a remarkable dry sense of humor, had helped me through many challenges. Around the same time and for no obvious reason, I also began to think about Fred Rogers. I met Mr. Rogers years ago when he baptized a child at our church, and I have been in awe of his deep understanding of children for years. His ability to bring calmness to any situation with very simple phrases and actions was extraordinary. Like my friend, Mr. Rogers exhibited deep, sincere concern for others and a very controlled ego. The examples of my friend and Mr. Rogers did not directly impact my personal fears or give me any insight into my troubled state of mind. Nevertheless, thinking about them helped to turn me away from my increasingly serious self-absorption. I decided on a whim to emulate Mr. Rogers as part of my new life after the diagnosis, even down to zippered sweaters (which may be easier to take on and off with increasing disability).

May 2012: Back to Maine. Zippered sweaters fit well in Maine. Each year we return to Maine in May to open our house for the season. That May, I very much wanted to return. Maine has always renewed my spirit, and I was much in need of renewal. At the same time, I was very anxious about my ability to tolerate the long drive. I was unsure about the impact of stress on my driving skills. I was also concerned about the occasional confusion I was experiencing, especially when tired. I talked about my concerns with Doug, who felt I could handle the trip. While I was not entirely convinced, Janet and I prepared to our drive to Maine in late May.

The drive turned out to be uneventful. My fears about my capabilities proved to be unfounded. Janet was more than able to adapt to my new limitations, driving nine of fourteen hours, spread over two days. While her new, expanded share of the driving duties contradicted my long-held self-image of myself as the marathon driver of our family, Janet had always enjoyed driving. I suspect she secretly welcomed longer stints behind the wheel. She certainly had more endurance than I. After driving one three-hour leg of our first nine-hour day, I was completely spent by the end of the day, while Janet was seemingly unfazed.

Mr. Rogers Lends a Hand. One of our escapes on a long road trip is to listen to an audio book over the course of the drive. For our trip that May, Janet had happened upon what appeared to be an interesting audio book at our local branch of the Carnegie Library. The author, a newspaper reporter, was befriended by Fred Rogers after he interviewed Rogers for an article. The relationship did not involve either work or common friends, and grew only from telephone calls, letters and occasional visits. By his own account, the friendship became profoundly significant for the author as he watched his brother's slow and difficult death at age 40.

The book caught my attention. I needed to be reminded that my current Parkinson's symptoms were trivial in comparison to a lingering, painful death at age 40. The challenges I faced were not so unusual or severe when compared with challenges faced every day by so many people. The book also reminded me that many of the most significant contributions I have made to the lives of others have had little or nothing to do with my work as a lawyer. Even chance conversations with friends or strangers can provide opportunities to be useful. If I could no longer be a lawyer, I could still help with a kind word, a word of encouragement or sometimes a word that triggers a new insight. Even though I was no longer a lawyer, I could still contribute to the welfare of friends, acquaintances and even strangers.

As I listened to the book with Janet, I recalled what I had initially thought to be a whim, to emulate Fred Rogers. Thinking more deeply about Fred Rogers' work, I remembered that he had said important things simply, often using stories and examples rather than narrative explanations to bring his point home. In the midst of my depression and confusion, stories and examples spoke to me at a more fundamental level than narrative explanations. Much like a Mr. Rogers' Neighborhood episode, the example of my old friend, the encouragement of people who understood my circumstances, and the few simple, unsophisticated ideas that had found resonance for me had, almost imperceptibly, begun to dispel the fog of my depression. Professional and polished expressions of sympathy or concern had done little for me, but the examples of my friends, the lives of others and their stories had reminded me how to live.

Maine has been an important part of our family life for over twenty-five years. Janet and I brought our children here every August as they were growing up. Our youngest child went to college here. It is a happy, almost magical place for me, filled with memories. The simple act of entering Maine had always raised my spirits. I hoped that this visit would likewise dispel my depression. It helped but could not dispel it completely. While our homecoming to Maine that May was sweet, it also underscored how many of the simple things that I had loved to do, like climbing, biking and hiking, I now would never do the same way again. Our youngest, Sare, joined us on the last leg of our drive and spent the next week with us at our home in Bernard. The generosity of time together helped to counteract my growing self-absorption. Janet, Sare and I hiked trails together through pine-infused woods and shared several memorable meals. I appreciated their company, the hikes and the food, but my appreciation was muted. I was still detached, passive and unable to express my gratitude fully, even though I knew I had every reason to be overwhelmingly grateful for their help and love.

PART II: Coming to Terms

Chapter 8: My First Parkinson's Buddy. Evolving Hopes and Fears

My First Parkinson's Buddy. A few days after our arrival in Maine, I picked up my camera and set off toward the harbor to try and find a good picture in the late afternoon light. On my walk I met a longtime summer resident that I had said hello to before, but never spoken to at any length. I surprised myself by telling him about my Parkinson's, violating my resolution to talk about Parkinson's only with old friends. He responded by telling me that his son-in-law, Gerry, also had Parkinson's, and happened to be visiting. Our conversation led to an introduction and an invitation to dinner. Gerry is a few years older than I am and was diagnosed seven years before me. We talked at length about Pittsburgh (our shared hometown), our shared interest in architecture and the challenges of Parkinson's. His sense of humor was robust. He was an engaging conversationalist. We made friends immediately.

Making friends with Gerry and his wife helped me to understand my future with Parkinson's more than all of the conversations I had with specialists and all that I had read. Gerry and his wife were coping with the symptoms of the disease and the side effects of the drugs seven years after his diagnosis. The challenge was significant, but they had adapted to their new reality. They were still working and traveling. They could still laugh. If my Parkinson's followed the same course, I reasoned, perhaps I could too.

The friends we have in Maine all share our love for the beauty of our island and the ocean that surrounds it. Perhaps as a result of this shared affection, or Maine's slower, more contemplative pace, or perhaps because I was simply growing less sensitive, I found it easier to talk about my Parkinson's with my friends in Maine than I had in Pittsburgh. Talking about the disease with friends over a quiet dinner helped me to remember what would have been obvious to me before my diagnosis. I was still me. I was still a useful and valued friend. While acquaintances might be uncomfortable with my symptoms and have little interest in a retired lawyer, my close friends would continue to accept me and value my friendship regardless of my symptoms or my retirement. Seeing how little my Parkinson's meant to them touched me far more than any expression of concern or sympathy I had received, no matter how sincere. I slowly began to accept that our cherished friends in Pittsburgh, Maine and elsewhere would not abandon me simply because of my Parkinson's.

My Rats Evolve. When friends objected to my rat analogy (too dark, they told me), I began to reconsider the image of virtual rodents chewing on the insulation that wrapped the wiring in my brain. The black humor still appealed to me, but the analogy was not entirely consistent with my growing experience. The virtual rodents were still chewing, but my neurological deterioration did not feel like a series of blown fuses as each new wire shorted out. The lights were not going off in sequence. Some days I felt my deterioration acutely. On others, I felt almost normal. When I was tired or stressed, my symptoms were marked and alarming. When I was rested and calm, I improved. I needed a new metaphor that took these variations into account. Perhaps some rodent exterminators were at work too. Perhaps my brain had enough plasticity to allow it to mitigate some of the damage the rats were doing. Perhaps stress reduction exercises could help me cope day by day. Could some of this be a reason for hope?

Our time in Maine that spring had helped me put some of my most irrational fears aside, but it did not dispel my depression. I was still discouraged and distinctly aware that Parkinson's threatened to deprive me of my ability to enjoy sensory experiences I had come to cherish and to rob me of my intellect in the offing. My fear had dulled with the passage of time, but the basic issues of mortality and loss were still lurking, waiting for my next crisis. When we returned to Pittsburgh in early June, I realized that the limited progress I had made was still fragile and at risk of being engulfed by my next wave of depression and stress. It was time to take a closer look at antidepressants.

My first brain drug. A surprising number of Americans take antidepressants every day. Most mental health professionals, including my neuropsychologist, believe firmly in their efficacy. However, brain scientists no longer subscribe to the theories that underpinned their original development, and indeed some studies suggest that antidepressants are only slightly more effective than a placebo. Beyond these uncertainties, I was reluctant to take a synthetic drug designed to penetrate my blood-brain barrier. Anti-depressants were yet another variable to introduce into my deteriorating brain. What new side effects would I discover? Would the drug help me, or would it introduce new, confusing, drug-induced symptoms?

Discouragement with my slow progress finally overcame my reluctance. I accepted the probability that my depression was too entrenched to be routed by exercise and the passage of time alone. I decided to try antidepressants. My doctors recommended that I first try citalopram, an antidepressant sold under the tradename "Celexa", which would change the way my brain used serotonin. I took their advice. We decided to begin the drug in mid-June on a date when I expected to be in Pittsburgh for at least six weeks. I started with one tablet on June 13. Not surprisingly, nothing happened. There were no immediate side effects, and no immediate relief. The next day was my sixtieth birthday. We celebrated as a family with a shared magnum of a delightful 1982 Bordeaux (stellar year, middling chateau). I went to bed at 11 p.m. that night, still basking in the lingering warmth of my family's love and a classic Bordeaux.

I did not bask for long. I woke at 2 a.m. with my pulse racing. My mouth was dry and filled with a distinctly metallic taste. I was frightened and anxious, even though I knew that these symptoms were almost certainly temporary side effects of the citalopram. As I did my best to moderate my fear, it occurred to me that perhaps my initial reservations about antidepressants were right. By morning, the symptoms had abated. I called Doug for advice, but in the short time before he could return my call, I realized the true source of my distress. Antidepressants might not be more effective than a placebo, but I am certain that they are far more incompatible with alcohol than any placebo could ever be, and their side effects are very real. Mixing citalopram with wine triggered what seemed to me at the time to be every side effect mentioned in the literature, and perhaps several more unknown to science. I sheepishly confessed my wine consumption to Doug, who to my chagrin pointed out again the warnings clearly printed on the citalopram pamphlet.

I love wine. It has been a shared hobby for Janet and me for the last thirty years and one of the ways we practice hospitality. The prospect of a life without wine was in itself depressing. Nonetheless, I had no appetite for further exploration of the dark side of antidepressants. I would mourn the deletion of wine from my diet, but I had no desire to mix wine and citalopram again, and it looked like I would be taking citalopram for the rest of my life.

Everything changes again. Five years is not long enough. Dan, my son in law, could not attend my birthday dinner, but did arrive the next day. He and Emily made an announcement that instantly put "the rest of my life" in an entirely different light and completely overshadowed my concerns about wine. Emily was pregnant. Now, as a grandparent to be, a five-year window seemed entirely inadequate. It looked like I still had work to do. Within a few weeks of that birthday, my periods of clarity seemed more frequent. I hoped that my increased exercise, a new sense of purpose and citalopram, individually or collectively, were beginning to have an impact on my depression. I still had not fully regained my interest in life or my energy and I often had days where the depression and fear returned with a vengeance, but the good days gave me hope that depression was not my new normal. My ability to tolerate noise, crowds and stress continued to deteriorate. My tremor worsened. My gait was sometimes imbalanced. I sometimes pulled to one side, raising concern about my ability to stay on sidewalks. My vision was still frequently blurred, often resulting in what I perceived internally (and unpleasantly) as two different, simultaneous images. These vision problems compounded the problems with my gait because I could not always see my path clearly. Overstimulation overwhelmed me, resulting in bouts of confusion and anxiety. Stress undermined my emotional control, resulting in inappropriate expressions of anger and frustration. My attention span often could be measured in minutes, if not seconds. I had little energy, and no hope of tackling the complex problems that had been my daily lot as a lawyer for over thirty years. The citalopram was a welcome help, but it was not going to restore everything.

I met with my neurologist for the second time on June 29. The office renovations that I had navigated in February were complete. Patients sat in a waiting room, no longer relegated to a chair in the hallway. My neurologist again collected me, this time from the renovated waiting room, and brought me to an examination room. As before, he watched me walk down the hall, wave my hands and tap my fingers. When we returned to the exam room, he told me that my motor symptoms had worsened, but not significantly.

Unlike my first visit, I now had questions to ask that I had been mulling over for months. We first discussed when I should start taking dopamine and what form it should take. I expressed a desire to defer the drugs because I thought that they would only work for a limited time, and delaying their use might extend their effectiveness. He explained that this was a misconception. The drugs would work until my dopamine production dropped to a level that made them ineffective. This would happen regardless of when I started to take the drugs. Despite his assurance, I was still reluctant to take new drugs. I was still secretly hoping that I would enjoy the full five drug-free years he had mentioned during my February appointment. I was likewise concerned about side effects. We ultimately agreed to defer the question of new drugs for six months.

We talked about my meeting with Tim Greenamyre. He agreed with Tim's observation that I could have 20 years or more of active life ahead. Perhaps I needed to hear it from my own doctor, or perhaps, because of the cumulative impact of all the assurances I had been given, I finally admitted to myself that my fixation on a five-year window was a distortion of what I had been told in my first exam.

Enrolling in SPARX. Some of my friends had urged me to participate in medical studies to learn more about my Parkinson's and to help advance Parkinson's care. When my neurologist had finished his examination and answered my questions about Parkinson's drug therapies, I asked about Parkinson's studies at UPMC. He said there were several studies that I might be interested in and introduced me to Larry, a UPMC colleague who managed Parkinson's research projects from an office a few doors down the hall. Larry told me with some enthusiasm about an ongoing study called SPARX, which focused on the impact of vigorous aerobic exercise during the early stages of Parkinson's. The study required an initial screening interview, which I completed before I left. It included a series of questions that dealt with other diseases and conditions that I might have in addition to my Parkinson's, such as heart disease, multiple sclerosis and cancer. The length of the list surprised me. I had been so focused on Parkinson's that I had thought of little else. The list was a graphic reminder that I was still prey to virtually every disorder known to medicine, and perhaps a few more. In other words, nothing had changed.

The SPARX study required some participants to exercise on a treadmill four times a week, each time maintaining a heart rate of 80 to 90% of their cardiac capacity for a minimum of thirty minutes. I have exercised regularly for years (with occasional lapses), but I had always avoided the treadmill. I was not sure that I could exercise at the required intensity on a new machine. Physical training was nothing new for me, but the high intensity training required by SPARX was. Nonetheless, I signed up for the SPARX study and scheduled a start time for the fall. I could spend the summer training in preparation.

Travel helped find the new me. By the start of summer, in spite of exercise and some help from the antidepressant, I was still periodically confused and terrified, still depressed. My initial coping strategies had failed. I was left with a simple desire to live each day fully, emulating Mr. Rogers as best I could, but was it enough? As it happened, a new challenge presented itself almost immediately. Janet and I have been avid travelers for most of our lives. As a student, travel meant freedom and excitement. As I grew older, I travelled to identify and explore my own tastes and preferences. At its best, travel allowed me a glimpse of what is important and true and beautiful in the world and an opportunity to avoid what is not. Over the years, travel matured me, gave me confidence, widened my horizon, and enriched my life.

Before the shadow of my Parkinson's fell over our plans, Janet and I looked forward to a retirement filled with travel. By July, however, my enthusiasm for travel had all but disappeared. I was no longer confident that I could cope with the physical rigors and stress of travel. I worried about luggage and the unavoidable crowding encountered in airplanes and with tour groups. I worried that my balance was not always reliable. I worried about fatigue. Beneath all of these practical concerns was anxiety about the unexpected stress of travel. I had no idea how I would react if we encountered any serious problem, let alone an accident or sickness.

Janet and I had booked a cruise in the Baltic nearly nine months before my diagnosis. We were to embark from Copenhagen in July in the company of old friends and sail north to St. Petersburg and then back to Stockholm with visits to Helsinki and Tallinn along the way. My anxiety mounted as our departure date approached. I became so indecisive that I seriously considered cancelling my reservation and encouraging Janet to go without me. At Janet's urging, I shared my concerns with Doug Reiss during our next regular session. He recommended that I go through with our travel plans, reminding me that we would be on a cruise ship, and not driving from hotel to hotel. I would be able to control the distance I would walk each day. I could even stay behind and rest if necessary. Moreover, our friends and the cruise staff could help with luggage and any unpleasant surprises.

In the end, we decided to go in spite of my worries. My decision was sealed not by arguments, but by Sare, our youngest, who offered to meet us in Prague and spend a few days exploring Prague and Berlin after our cruise. It was an offer I could not refuse. I was happy to face the challenges and risks of travel with Parkinson's for an opportunity to explore two new cities with Janet and Sare. We had enjoyed travel time together many times in the past, and this might be a last time. With some lingering trepidation, we boarded a plane to meet our friends in Copenhagen a few days before the cruise, just as we had planned to do months before.

It turned out, not surprisingly, my fears about travel were entirely overblown. I still had the ability to function fine even in the face of simple travel mishaps. For example, while in flight from Pittsburgh to Newark, we learned that a fire in the Newark airport tower would delay our flight. Rather than fret about connections, as I would have done before my diagnosis, I refused to speculate about the impact of the delay. With a little deep breathing, I was able to disengage and avoid the confusion and anxiety that might otherwise have undone me. For the remainder of the trip, Janet and our friends steered me away from potentially stressful situations and were gracious when I needed a break or a nap. As for more difficult challenges, Janet was quick to take over when she sensed that I was likely to be overwhelmed.

At each port we took advantage of the excursions offered by the cruise line. All of the excursions involved walking. My energy level was often low, but I took naps in the afternoon and sometimes sat while Janet shopped or explored with our friends. I was easily winded and rested often, but I never fell seriously behind our group. In retrospect, falling behind should never have been a concern. Most cruises are designed for the newly retired, and fitness is often elusive in this demographic.

Our cruise ended in Stockholm. We had arranged before the tour to visit a relative who had moved to Stockholm in the eighties to marry a business school classmate and stayed to raise his family. (I will call our Stockholm relative Stan to protect his privacy.) I was particularly interested in spending some time with Stan because of his experience with Parkinson's. Stan's father had been diagnosed with Parkinson's when he was in his sixties. Although living in Sweden at the time, Stan had followed the progression of his father's disease from his early symptoms through his death.

Stan's father had been a highly successful businessman. I had found him to be charming, outgoing, energetic and intelligent. My symptoms seemed to parallel his early symptoms. He had always been physically active, and he coped with the symptoms well for a time. However, he gradually became discouraged as his problems with movement, speech and swallowing multiplied. Parkinson's drugs eventually became ineffective for him, just as they be will for me. In the end, Stan's father developed a sharp pain in his abdomen. The pain was unrelenting and did not respond to treatment. After weeks (or perhaps months), he turned to hospice for palliative care and stopped eating. He did not discuss his decision to turn to hospice care with his son, who was still researching Parkinson's therapies when his father died.

Stan and I met years after his father's death, but when we spoke, it was apparent that he was not entirely at peace with his father's decision. Stan could not understand why his father had decided to surrender his life to escape the disease at a time when Stan believed that hope still remained. Thinking about Stan's father, I could easily imagine an accumulation of increasingly challenging symptoms that would in time be simply overwhelming, particularly if I were convinced that the symptoms were irreversible. I could also understand a decision to end one's life before the pain and disability became intractable, let alone afterward. I suspect that many secretly choose this route as their Parkinson's progresses to avoid what they see as unnecessary suffering.

Turning to hospice care may well have been the best choice that Stan's father had among the handful of hard choices left to him. There may have been little reason for him to prolong his suffering, particularly if he had unbearable pain and believed that his decline would be progressive with no hope of improvement. In the end, his decision to seek hospice care was his decision alone. At the same time, his decision continued to have serious implications for his family long after his death. Stan was still grappling with unanswered questions raised by his father's choice two decades later.

There was much in my talks with Stan that made me uncomfortable. It is one thing to read about symptoms that have been suffered by strangers and it is something else again to hear the stories of a relative who has witnessed the actual decline and ultimate surrender of a parent. It is easy to discount the experiences of anonymous strangers. It is easy and convenient to assume that strangers are different than we are; we tell ourselves that we are healthier, we have resources they do not; we are smarter about our care; we have more family support; and we therefore can convince ourselves that we are on a completely different path. Stan's father was not a stranger, and I had no basis to assume that my Parkinson's would follow a materially different course than his. Denial is difficult to maintain in the face of unavoidable concrete reality.

Stan's reaction to his father's reticence confirmed my decision to share my experience with the disease with my family. I do not want to leave unanswered questions for my children, and I want them to learn from my experience. I do not want my children to believe that denial is an appropriate or effective way to face their own challenges. Moreover, perhaps both my children and I can tame our unspoken fears by talking about things that my fathers' generation so carefully suppressed.

Stan and his wife were enormously generous with their time during our visit. Their hospitality and charm and the delights of their city gave me room to defer thoughts about the difficult parts my conversations with Stan for the rest of our trip. While I was pleasantly entertained by the distractions of travel, I knew that I could not ignore my future indefinitely.

After our farewells to family and friends in Stockholm, we flew to Prague to meet Sare. We found Prague to be a storybook city, having largely escaped the dual depredations of war and progress that ravaged so many beautiful European cities in the twentieth century. Berlin, by contrast, was enormous and filled with young trees and new buildings, a cutting-edge city where few vestiges of life before 1945 remain. Both cities were filled with ghosts. In Prague I thought about Kafka and in Berlin, the appalling worldwide calamities that were nurtured and meticulously managed there, and the worldwide retribution that followed, so great in scope that it drew my father to Europe before I was born and left Berlin a massive mound of dust and rubble. My Parkinson's pales to insignificance in the face of unimaginable suffering on such a massive scale. After less than a week, we were all ready to come home.

Confronting reality We returned to Pittsburgh from Berlin in July. Because we had no pressing obligations to keep us in Pittsburgh, we decided to drive back to Maine in early August and stay until early September. I was looking forward to my chair at the corner of the porch and an opportunity to sort through my thoughts and the photographs from our trip. I was tired from the trip, but I did not often feel the full weight of depression that I had carried in February and March. The depression and anxiety were still there, but they had given up their exclusive claim to center stage.

When we left Pittsburgh for Copenhagen in June, the trip had seemed both too self-indulgent and too challenging. After we returned, I realized that both of these perspectives were inaccurate. We did not travel to the Baltic in pursuit of sybaritic excess (although some may have occurred). We traveled to meet new people, to learn new things, to see places we have studied, to challenge our prejudices, and to celebrate life with people we love, and that is what we did. The trip was not physically demanding, and we were able to gradually make accommodations to my Parkinson's when required.

Instead of generating stress, the entire trip turned out to be therapeutic. It gave me a way to loosen the bonds of self-absorption that had fed my depression after the diagnosis. New sensory experiences cut through my depression-induced apathy and allowed me to focus more on the present and distance myself from my uncertain future. Forgotten, familiar and new textures, aromas, and sensations rekindled my appreciation of food and helped to turn my attention back to the simple, immediate sensory experience of life. Each day Janet, Sare and our friends showed me that I could still be a blessing to those around me. While my enthusiasm was still constrained by my continuing depression, travel had reminded me that there were still things in life that could engage my spirit and my intellect.

In the weeks following our return from Berlin, I became increasingly convinced that Parkinson's, or at least my reaction to it, had been distorting my thinking for some time. I began to see my Parkinson's as a cunning liar that had shouldered its way into my inner dialogue, intent upon undermining my confidence, slowing my thinking and sowing confusion. I was not dying, as my Parkinson's would have me believe. Nothing of significance had yet changed that would call for any real limits on my activities. If I could free myself from fear and shake my depression, I still had the capacity to live a full life, at least for a time. That time may be short or it may be long. Neither I nor anyone else can know what the next day or hour or second will bring. Because I can only live today, I need to live today as best I can. To do that, I need to be a blessing.

In short, nothing has changed. Carpe diem.

In August 2012, Janet and I contemplated trying another trip. We were invited to join a group from our church that was going to visit seminaries and churches in China's Shandong Province in late October. The two-week trip would start in Shanghai and end in Bejing, with site visits in Shanghai, Jinan and Weihai. It would provide a view of China that few Americans have seen. I very much wanted to go on the trip with Janet but was again concerned about my ability to meet the demands of travel.

The trip was almost certain to involve moments of significant stress and likely would tax me both physically and intellectually far more than our Baltic cruise had done. Just as in the Baltic, though, Janet would be by my side to intercede when I was overwhelmed, and we would be among friends who were sensitive to my limitations. Air quality in China can reach dangerous levels and would normally have been a serious concern, but we would be visiting during a weeklong national holiday when factories would be closed. Pollution would likely be tolerable. On balance, the chance to see a side of China few visitors see outweighed the likely risks.

Janet and I boarded a plane bound for Shanghai in early October. We had decided to break up the long flight by leaving from San Francisco rather than Pittsburgh. We also added a day at the beginning of the trip to allow us time to rest before we joined our group. The stopover and extra day may have reduced my jet lag somewhat, but the lack of sleep and extended inactivity during the flight still left me groggy, stiff, and slow moving and slow-witted. Apparently, I did not leave my Parkinson's at home. Nearly everywhere we went in China was crowded. Nearly everyone we encountered was friendly. Construction was booming in the cities, and small street businesses were everywhere. Industry was the order of the day. In large cities, we were ignored. In small cities, apart from an occasional mistrustful stare from older onlookers, we were merely a curious oddity. Communism had receded. In its stead, technocrats managed the country with eyes locked on commerce and the future. Even the tanks on Tiananmen Square in 1989 had been conveniently forgotten by virtually everyone in China. History and propaganda had become one.

The seminaries and churches we visited seemed very similar to Protestant seminaries and churches in United States and the rest of the world. By 2012 China had grown increasingly tolerant of Christianity. This new tolerance had limits. All churches still existed at the pleasure of the government. A misstep could still result in a church's loss of necessary licenses and permits. Churches were growing quickly. In less than a generation, there will likely be more Christians in China than in the United States. Of course, even then Christians would still be a tiny minority completely at the mercy of a government not known for mercy.

Janet and I planned to stay in Beijing for several days after the rest of our group returned home. We wanted to see the Summer Palace and other historic sites at our own pace. While visiting the national art museum, I was distracted and failed to notice that the wide, uniformly lit, perfectly white marble stairway at the entrance to the museum consisted of not one, but two sets of stairs and no handrails. The second set of steps came as a complete surprise. As best as I can recall, I fell about four feet and landed on my knee and shin. Janet and a security guard helped me to a bench. After resting for a half hour, I hobbled to a taxi and we returned to our hotel.

The next day my knee was stiff and throbbing. A kind receptionist at our hotel gave me an ice pack and lent me a cane. With the assistance of many people, we managed the flight home without further mishap. Full recovery took over six weeks. Nothing was broken, but the message was clear. This would not be my last fall.

Neither my fall nor the likelihood of future falls dampened my renewed enthusiasm for travel. Travel had helped me to ignore for a time Parkinson's likely impact on my future. The fatigue and depression felt less pronounced while we were traveling. Planning possible future trips gave me hope for the future. Seeing more of the world reminded me how small and unimportant my personal concerns were. As important as travel was to me, my fall in the Chinese museum was a clear reminder that my ability to travel could end in a moment with little or no warning. I'll go there "someday" now meant "probably not."

Closing-up shop. When we returned from China in late October, I could no longer ignore the need to close shop. My office lease would end in less than five months. Before I could close my office, I had to review and prepare twenty years of files for storage. The work was interminable, uninteresting, and unpaid. I did not have the energy to spend more than an hour or two on the files daily. Some days I could not work at all. The knee I injured in China was still painful and it made walking difficult. Thankfully, scans confirmed that my knee damage was not permanent.

By the time the fall gave way to winter, I had made noticeable progress in some areas. My symptoms were becoming more familiar and easier to manage, even though they slowly progressed. Janet was deftly steering me away from stressful events. My depression still lingered, but on Doug's recommendation, I increased my antidepressant dose, although the increase was slow to take hold. While my symptoms were not surprising, Parkinson's had lost none of its unpredictable intensity. It could still inspire abject existential terror without notice day or night, rob me of all my energy with no warning, and envelop me in a cloud of confusion and self-doubt, only to again recede into the background for several days.

Forced Exercise. Within a few months after my diagnosis, I had begun to hear from friends and acquaintances that intense exercise might help to slow the progression of my Parkinson's. While I was more than willing to start a new exercise program specifically focused on Parkinson's, no one seemed to know how much exercise or what kind of exercises were best. One neurologist reported in a speech available on the Internet that he had observed significant temporary improvement in a patient's physical symptoms after the patient rode on a tandem bike with a stronger and faster partner. It was unclear from the neurologist's explanation whether the necessary intensity could only be reached with help from a partner (such as the tandem bike rider) or whether it could be attained in a solitary workout. The term "forced exercise" cropped up in other places, but for me, all exercise is a bit forced.

Still, in spite of my worries about "forced", I was relieved to be was cleared to participate in the SPARX exercise study. Even better, I was assigned to a group that would exercise at what seemed to be the highest heart rates. The design of the study would give me a sense of what exercise levels are most helpful. The emphasis on heart rate in the study confirmed my suspicion that intensity and "forced exercise" meant a focus on cardiovascular training. After passing a stress test required for participation, I was scheduled to start monitored exercise sessions in early November. The drill was familiar. Like all aerobic exercise programs, the study recommend exercise to a heart rate in the range of 80% to 90% of heart capacity for at least half an hour, preceded by a warmup and followed by a cool down.

At first I exercised at a UPMC facility under the supervision of a physical therapist temporarily enlisted to serve as my minder. For several weeks, the therapist stood beside the treadmill to monitor my heart rate and gait and to intercede if I was about to shoot off the back of the treadmill, have a heart attack, or succumb from excessive boredom. Boredom turned out not to be a problem even though the treadmill work was hard and monotonous. A regular conversation with my therapist minder helped me to explore the physical problems I was beginning to experience, particularly with my gait. Over the course of about a month, my supervised sessions dropped to once a month and I returned to my home gym to complete my weekly exercises free of supervision.

It was quickly apparent that I had not been honest with myself about the intensity and consistency of my past exercise habits. Initially, I found it difficult to exercise four days a week at the intensity level required by the study. When I had used exercise machines before the study, my heart rate would reach desired levels after an appropriate warm up, but my attention would wander and my heart rate slip gradually lower. Maintaining a high heart rate required constant attention. This was no surprise. Done correctly, exercise is hard physical work. I might have dropped out of the SPARX program in the first month had it not been for my growing awareness that exercise was helping, at least a little. Also I had made a commitment when I signed up for the study. To fulfill the letter and spirit of my commitment and to get as much benefit from exercise as I could, I decided to give exercise the same priority as I had given my legal work before I closed my office. Exercise could no longer be sacrificed to allow time for other pursuits. Since I was no longer doing any legal work, save for true emergencies, exercise had first claim on my time. For lack of a better description of my new, exercise-first persona, I began to tell people that I left the practice of law to become a professional exerciser.

By the close of 2012, my life had settled into a weekly routine. Four to six days a week I would go to the gym in the morning. Once there, I would stretch, jog two miles on a treadmill, and do body weight resistance exercises for 45 minutes. Sometimes I would do yoga poses. On typical Mondays I met with my trainer for an hour to improve my form. On Fridays, I attended an intermediate yoga class. On both these days I also walked two miles on the treadmill.

My transition from lawyer to professional exerciser happened gradually. At first, I found forced exercise to be daunting. Warm-up exercise took ten to fifteen minutes instead of the five minutes that I had needed to warm up ten years earlier. Fatigue was a constant companion. I almost always needed a nap after exercise and practically collapsed into bed at night.

Benefits followed. The walking steadily grew more tolerable over the first few months as I grew stronger and the exercise routine became an integral part of my day. After two months, exercise was firmly integrated into my daily schedule. After six months, I noticed growing relief from my depression. The gym staff and gym regulars provided the same daily, easy banter that I had enjoyed with my co-workers before I retired. The gym was beginning to feel like home.

Eventually I looked forward to my visits. I wanted to exercise. On days when I worked out, my mood was better. I was more engaged in the world around me; I was confused much less often. I could tolerate a limited amount of stress. However, there were limits. I was still plagued by fatigue. If I missed my exercise for more than a day or two, my symptoms would quickly return, largely unabated. Exercise, particularly high intensity aerobics (i.e., the SPARX program), was proving to be a potent drug with health benefits beyond my Parkinson's.

If intense exercise is a drug, it is not without side effects. Intense exercise goes hand in hand with minor injuries. Repetitive motion leads to inflammation. Forced exercise means pushing limits, and pushing limits increases the chances of falls, abrasions, and soft tissue injuries. I was therefore not particularly surprised when my regular sessions on the treadmill resulted in significant pain in the arch of my foot. The pain gave way to plantar fasciitis. My physical therapist minder suggested that the pain might be due to the fact that I used too steep a setting on the treadmill. I reduced the incline. The pain receded over several weeks.

After I moved to a flat treadmill, I increased my speed to a jog to maintain my heart rate. Soon my big toes became very sensitive to pressure, making it very difficult to walk. This time the cause was obvious but harder to address. My time on the treadmill had apparently inflamed arthritis in my toes. A physical therapist fashioned an orthotic insert for my shoe, while a podiatrist recommended that I switch from dress shoes to wide, low hiking shoes. An orthopedic surgeon recommended meloxicam to address pain and inflammation. I tried everything my doctors and therapists suggested and adopted the recommendations that seemed to work best.

Discovering Boxing. My SPARX-inspired regimen worked well for a while but the end of 2013, I became aware that my exercise program no longer had the kind of intensity needed to slow the pace of my worsening motor symptoms. Over the Christmas holiday, I had a chance conversation with Arthur, a friend who had returned to Pittsburgh to visit his family during the holidays. Arthur told me about Freddy Roach. Roach is one of the most successful boxing trainers on the West Coast. He continued to train elite boxers even though he has had Parkinson's for nearly thirty years. In interviews, Roach claimed that the rigorous training routines he uses with his boxers slowed the progression of his Parkinson's symptoms. His claim was particularly plausible. Boxing training is among the most demanding in all of sports. Boxing was nothing if not forced exercise.

I was once told that Michael Fox has recommended that newly diagnosed Parkinson's patients take up a new sport after their diagnosis, preferably one that they know little or nothing about. I assume that he recommends a new sport to avoid the frustration of slowly losing hard-won and still valued skills and to encourage the brain to remap itself by acquiring new ways of moving. From this perspective, boxing was a perfect new sport for me. I knew nothing about it. I had never watched a fight, not even on television. Perhaps because

I knew nothing about boxing, I was curious. A little research quickly brought me to Nelson Mandela's biography. Mandela credited boxing as the inspiration for the strategies he employed against South Africa's Apartheid system. Mandela would first assess his opponent by direct attack, probing with jabs and footwork. If the opponent was too strong, he would switch to a defensive strategy, hoping his stamina exceeded that of his opponent.

In the matter of Apartheid, the strategy ultimately worked, although, for Mandela, victory came at a frightful personal cost. I have been for some time in awe of Mandela's courage, his faith in his cause, his persistence in opposing injustice, and his unbending integrity. If he learned any of this from boxing, I needed no other confirmation of the value of the sport for me.

Fortuitously, my fitness club added boxing to its fitness offerings in 2013. Tom Yankello, a well-known Western Pennsylvania trainer, was giving private boxing lessons one day a week. Tom had been a highly successful boxer and continued to train professional boxers at his boxing gym near Pittsburgh. I promptly signed up.

Boxers train intensively because boxing demands intensity. A boxing match consists of 15 three-minute rounds, each followed by a one-minute break. In every round, the boxers experience heart rates at or near their maximum heart rate. Dopamine release is sure to follow.

I fell into a new rhythm. Many things have helped. Sometimes exercise is a distraction. Somedays it genuinely feels like a treatment. Boxing is increasingly available for Parkinson's patients through the Rock Steady Boxing program. I have become a regular and a supporter and continue to make new friends through the Rock Steady program. Boxing was a discovery for me in year two after my diagnosis, and years later I am still grateful for what it has brought to my life, exercise and companionship. People are the essential link. More about this in the next chapters.

PART III: LOOKING FORWARD

Exercise was helping. In the two years following my diagnosis, my feelings of shame had faded, and my depression gradually lifted somewhat. Nevertheless, my comfort in social interaction was slower to return. I no longer thought that my death was imminent, but I was acutely aware of my growing disability. I never knew when my voice would fail me or when I would lose my train of thought. My gait was deteriorating. I did not know when my periodic bouts of confusion would begin or, once begun, when they would pass. I never knew when my bladder would present me with an immediate, non-negotiable demand. All of these symptoms could be socially awkward, and any one or a combination of several could occur without warning. I was comfortable with small groups of friends and family, but avoided crowds and strangers. Noise and crowds first made me uncertain and tentative, and then brought on tremors and confusion.

Retirement compounded my social discomfort. My legal work had brought me into regular contact with people, provided predictable topics of conversation, and generated a stream of interesting stories. It gave me confidence. It gave me an identity. Now, I did not even know whether to tell people I was disabled or retired. I had no new stories and the most interesting parts of my days involved exercise, a poor basis for conversation at best. I was becoming socially invisible. I could not speak fast enough to participate in a fast-moving conversation. My comedic timing was just a few beats off, just enough to make an apt comment mildly uncomfortable. I felt that I had little to contribute to social conversation. It seemed that I had given up my place in the world, and I had lost my voice in the offing.

These feelings were not new to me. I recalled a similar but much more intense feeling of having lost my place in the world in1980 when my first wife died suddenly and unexpectedly. Then as now, what I believed to be normal life seemed to vanish. It was as if all color drained from the world in an instant and no one else seemed to notice. I was depressed, angry, and confused. I had no idea what would become of me. Then as now, I was distinctly uncomfortable among members of the healthy world, the world of people who were not grieving. It seemed incongruous that the world could still function as if nothing had happened, while I was bereft. During the depths of my grief, I sensed a profound emotional gulf between those who are grieving and those who are not. Before my wife died, I was an enthusiastic citizen of the healthy world. The disabled and simply ill rarely entered my field of vision. When I did encounter them, I was always polite, but often found little to talk about. I would perhaps offer encouragement, but I did not encourage sincere and intimate conversation. I did not want to be drawn into a conversation. Before my wife died, I could be polite and solicitous with friends and acquaintances in crisis, but I could not speak intelligently or even helpfully about their experience. More importantly, I was afraid of their suffering. As I grew more uncomfortable with healthy people, I grew more comfortable with people who also faced serious health problems.

When my wife died, I knew immediately that I was grieving. Then, my feeling of loss was obvious, raw, immediate and overwhelming, just as it had been when my father had died a year earlier. Despite my past familiarity with grief, it took months for me to recognize that some of the most painful feelings triggered by my Parkinson's diagnosis involved feelings of grief. I was grieving loss, this time not of a cherished spouse or a parent, but of cherished expectations for my future. I learned several hard lessons from my personal grief as a young widower. Grief can be postponed or even suppressed for a time, but it will almost invariably return in an unpredictable and damaging way if it is not allowed to run its natural course. Grief will not succumb to suppression, denial or any of the myriad of psychological ploys I have tried in unsuccessful attempts to avoid unavoidable pain. Grief cannot be rushed. I had moments of intense sadness and loss for years after my wife died. They grew more infrequent as the years passed, but my memory of them remains.

The grief I felt over the loss of my future hopes was mild in comparison to the grief I felt when my wife and parents died, but the fear was much stronger. Even two years after my diagnosis I would still wake to moments of mortal terror. Janet has become my strongest source of comfort.

On the day my Parkinson's was diagnosed, Janet and I had been married for over twenty-five years. Our marriage had been and continued to be happy and fruitful, despite (or perhaps because of) the unexpected calamities and challenges that we weathered together over its course. Shared faith, values, and goals combined with years of shared responsibility for our three children, life experience and love gradually transformed us from two single parents into what has been an effective and durable partnership. Even in the depths of my depression, I had no doubt that we could face my Parkinson's together. More importantly, I knew from long experience that Janet would stand by me, no matter what might befall us.

While my confidence in Janet was based on our mutual love and shared experience, my Parkinson's diagnosis was unlike any other calamity we had yet faced in our time together. Six months after the diagnosis, Parkinson's had already begun to erode my ability to perform my share of household duties. I could no longer handle the stress of any unplanned contingency. My speech had slowed and my hearing had deteriorated. I was more forgetful. Depression made me a less engaging and engaged companion. I had no energy but could not sleep. I was growing physically and emotionally tentative. In short, I seemed to be developing all of the traits that wives find most frustrating in their aging husbands. My Parkinson's was impacting and would continue to impact Janet's life as profoundly as it was impacting mine. We were entering uncharted waters.

The depression that followed my diagnosis made me very emotional about my family and, most of all, about Janet. I felt extremely grateful for Janet's love and support and told her so often. Despite this, I soon developed the belief that I was not expressing myself adequately. We talked as often as we had talked in the past. I expressed my love in the same ways and if anything more frequently. Now, however, I also felt compelled to explain to Janet at every opportunity how difficult and frightening I found my symptoms. I felt that Janet could not understand my plight, having never experienced Parkinson's herself. Of course, I was wrong about the depth of her comprehension, but depression is impervious to facts and logic.

Janet always listened quietly and thoughtfully to my laments, but she wisely refused to be drawn into my growing self-absorption and nascent self-pity. She was consistently cheerful and supportive in the face of my emotional distress. She encouraged me to talk freely with her, but she neither accepted nor rejected my complaints. She continued to live her life as she always had. She saw her friends, worked on her projects and enjoyed her life. She even seemed to enjoy my company, at least when I was not completely mired in depression. Janet's constancy became a beacon for me, illuminating my way home.

For some time after my diagnosis, I was no longer the confident husband I had been just a few years earlier. I was acutely aware of a decline in my strength, balance and endurance. I could not keep up with Janet when we walked together. I could no longer play the role of a younger man; I could not manage the heavy lifting. I felt physically unattractive and diminished. By any objective standard, I was.

In the muddled state of mind that I often found myself in during the months following the diagnosis, I failed to consider that Janet had never given me any indication that my symptoms made me any less attractive to her. Slowly, Janet's constancy wore through the miasma of my self-absorption. I knew that Janet found me worthy of her love in spite of my shortcomings. She still found me attractive despite all the objective evidence to the contrary. No other opinion, especially mine, has any real significance to me, nor should it. If Janet finds me attractive, then I am.

Depression was not the only challenge that Parkinson's brought to our marriage. We knew from the start that Parkinson's would over time change the fundamental dynamics of our family. Parkinson's had already begun to transform my face into a mask and sap my strength. On any given day, it could imbalance my stride, soften my voice to a whisper, deprive me of my sense of smell or taste, or render me largely useless. It took no great feat of reasoning to realize that Parkinson's would gradually rob me of my ability to be as active a husband, father and soon-to-be grandfather as I had hoped to continue to be for at least another decade. It had begun.

Janet and I had forged an efficient and resilient partnership over twenty-five years of (apparently)

Parkinson's free marriage. Each of us had a deep and largely accurate understanding of the other's preferences, opinions, values, foibles, strengths, and weaknesses. Simple habits practiced over the course of many years were filled with special meaning that neither of us could express in words. In countless subtle, mostly non-verbal ways, we reassured, calmed, encouraged, protected, inspired, challenged, corrected and affirmed each other. A comfortable distribution of household responsibilities and financial control evolved slowly to meet changing circumstances. Parkinson's was a circumstance that would change the way we shared control and responsibility at a speed we had never anticipated or experienced in the past.

By the end of summer, Janet and I had begun to modify our partnership, or, more accurately, our partnership had begun to evolve in response to my symptoms. Janet assumed more responsibility for managing our finances. She cooked, as she always had, and I cleaned up. She worked harder to compensate for my changing role. Thankfully, the actual changes we made through the summer were incremental and far from overwhelming. Most of the early changes that we made in our marriage were made to reduce my stress levels. The most significant change involved my driving. After the diagnosis, my tremor sometimes made it difficult for me to drive smoothly. I also could become flustered in traffic. Watching me become flustered made Janet nervous. When Janet was visibly nervous, I became even more easily flustered. This emotional feedback loop often left me rattled, which of course led to mistakes that made Janet even more sensitive to my driving. By mid summer, Janet asked me not to drive while she was in the car. I acquiesced. Janet would now do most of the short trips and all the long distance driving that we had previously shared.

This change in our driving pattern resulted in an unexpected insight. After Janet began to do more of the driving, I realized that she still loved to drive as much as she had when we first met. My long-held assumption that she preferred to be a passenger on long trips was obviously as wrong as it was self-serving. She was happy to drive all of the time. More surprising to me, I was ready to enjoy a view of the countryside that I had largely ignored since I first obtained a driver's license at 16. I continued to drive when Janet was not in the car, but I was happy to be a navigator too.

I wondered about my unexpected willingness to limit my driving. If I could enjoy riding in a car that I did not control, perhaps I could relax my control over other areas of my life. Accepting limits on my control could make it easier to accept the limitations that Parkinson's would soon impose on me, and it could free me to focus on things that I really care about. If I can grow to accept the lack of control and heightened sense of vulnerability brought on by my Parkinson's, perhaps I might also grow to be a more sensitive and effective husband and father.

Financial setbacks heighten the marital stress that goes hand and hand with Parkinson's. Disability compounds financial stress. For the majority of people coping with Parkinson's, I suspect that money is a constant concern. There is no way to predict when Parkinson's evolving symptoms will further impinge upon my ability to drive, to walk, to live independently, or, for that matter, to perform any human function. Each stage in the development of the disease seems to introduce new expenses. Parkinson's will not submit to the discipline of a budget. I am grateful that, by the time of my diagnosis, our total savings and investments had grown to the point where I was reasonably confident that we could handle the future costs of dealing with my Parkinson's and still have a comfortable retirement, barring any additional calamities. I have enormous respect for everyone who faces Parkinson's alone or with limited financial resources.

There may come a time when I can no longer care for myself, and I will need to look to Janet for all my needs, but that time is not yet upon us. For some time, I have needed help with shirt buttons and stress avoidance. Janet is becoming increasingly adept at steering me away from stressful situations. The future will bring new challenges; some may overwhelm me. It makes no sense to anticipate the future course of my disease; there is, after all, no cure. I cannot predict where tomorrow will take me. If I put my mind to it, however, I have a shot at living well today.

The grandson that my daughter and son-in-law had announced back in June arrived on January 27, 2013. His parents named him West in honor of Janet's family. His arrival changed life for all of us, but for me, he was nothing less than a godsend. I was a granddad - Bappa in our family. From the moment I first looked at him eye to eye, I realized that I had a fundamental duty to nurture, protect and guide this newborn soul, and that I would owe this duty to him, and any future siblings and cousins, for the rest of my life.

I had struggled unsuccessfully after my retirement to find something that would help me recover the sense of direction and purpose that I lost when I stopped working. West, and all future grandchildren, have begun to fill that void. Janet and I would not in any way be the primary caregivers for our grandchildren, but we could provide the same experience, financial support, resolve that our grandparents freely bestowed on us and that our parents freely bestowed on our children. This was now our job; not a fulltime job, but one with meaning and purpose that would continue even in the face of my own disability and eventual death.

Our duty to our grandchildren was a blessing that Janet and I were, of course, pleased to embrace. We had long dreamed of introducing each of our grandchildren to the beauty and grandeur of Acadia, Yosemite, Jasper, Glacier and Yellowstone National Parks, and the nearly limitless wonders of travel. We wanted to share the adventures we had found only in books. We wanted them to drink deeply of the spirit of adventure, opportunity, generosity, fairness and integrity. We wanted to teach them about the importance humility, courage, patience, persistence and, most of all, love. We wanted them to be students familiar with the both the world of ideas and the world of action. There was much that we wanted to do with them, and, for my part, it had to be done while I still had the energy, strength, intelligence and dexterity to do it.

While my symptoms have continued to evolve, they also have grown more familiar. My early morning bouts of anxiety are less frequent, and will, I think, continue to recede, at least until my next close encounter with mortality. I had been able for most of my adult life to manage fears with the sheer weight of everyday life. When my workload lightened in retirement, my mind returned to these worries, and I realized that I could only continue to control my fear by facing it, and that I would never have a better chance to face my fear than now. One cannot live fully if living in fear of this disease. In the fall of 2014, a friend gave me a copy of this short poem:

We will die, but not today

We know far less than we think we do

Death is itself trivial – everyone does it

So, faith, friends and family continue to sustain me.

THE AUTHOR

The author is Edward Boss Wood, a retired attorney who practiced law in Pittsburgh, Pennsylvania for almost 40 years. He graduated from Washington and Jefferson College and University of Pittsburgh Law School. He is married to Janet Wood, the father of three children and grandfather of six. He has a wide variety of interests and is a skilled photographer. He now lives in Bernard, Maine.

Made in the USA
Middletown, DE
04 September 2024

60367394R00051